MO'S MISCHIEF

Best Mom Ever

Titles in the Mo's Mischief series:

Best Mom Ever
Four Troublemakers
Pesky Monkeys
Teacher's Pet

MO'S MISCHIEF

Best Mom Ever

Hongying Yang

HarperTrophy®
An Imprint of HarperCollinsPublishers

Mo's Mischief: Best Mom Ever
Text copyright © 2004 by Hongying Yang
English translation copyright © 2008 by HarperCollins Publishers
Illustrations copyright © 2004 by Pencil Tip Culture & Art Co.

Library of Congress catalog card number: 2008920941
ISBN 978-0-06-156475-8

❖

First published in China by Jieli Publishing House, 2004
First published in Great Britain by HarperCollins Children's Books, 2008
First U.S. Edition, 2008

A VERY SPECIAL MOM

Mo Shen Ma's weekend homework was to write an essay called "My Family Is Special."

Mo put up his hand. "Ms. Qin, there is *nothing* special about my family."

"Nonsense," Ms. Qin replied. "Every family is special for one reason or another. Think about something that only you know about your family; something really special; something none of your friends know about."

The boy who sat in front of Mo and who always acted a little too smart for his own good was Chao, better known by his nickname, Monkey. Monkey turned to Mo and whispered, "Ms. Qin must want some gossip about our families! She wants us to tell family secrets!"

Ms. Qin heard Monkey. She had very sharp hearing and missed nothing that happened in her class. Any student who tried to misbehave, or talked in class thinking they would not be caught, would be very sorry. . . .

"Monkey, you were up to your tricks again, weren't you?"

Monkey's "tricks" all involved talking—talking a lot of nonsense!

As soon as Mo got home from school, he wrote the title of his essay at the top of a clean piece of paper: "My Family Is Special."

But what could he write about?

There would be plenty of things to write about his father, who was definitely not like an average dad. But Mo couldn't write about his father, because his father was already a celebrity at the school. Everyone in school knew about Mo's father.

Whenever Mo got into trouble, Mr. Ma would come to school driving his custom-built SUV—the only car of its kind in the world. And it wasn't just his car that made him famous. Whenever he came to school, Mo's dad got himself into all kinds of hilarious situations. Stories about Mo's dad kept teachers and students entertained all year. Like the time he tried to drive his car through the school playground during a fire drill, or the time he came to school wearing his Grumpy costume after his office skit of *Snow White and the Seven Dwarves*. Then there was the time when he came into school wanting to try out the robot toys he was designing for his company, but the robot toys went completely out of control! No, Mo certainly couldn't write anything about his father for this essay.

Then Mo had an idea! He decided he would write about his mother. Ms. Qin was very curious to meet Mo's mother because she wanted to know whether she was as mischievous as her son and her husband. But Mo's mother had never visited the school—she was too scared of hearing bad things about her mischievous son!

 3

Ms. Qin had said by "special," she meant something that no one else knew about. Mo thought there were loads of things that other people didn't know about his mom. To begin with, there was her name!

Mo and his dad always called Mo's mother Honeybunch. But her *real* name was Blossom. Honeybunch was a nickname Mo's father made up because flower blossoms attract bees and bees make honey! Mr. Ma had once told his wife that even when his hair turned gray and he was covered in wrinkles, he would still call her Honeybunch. And like father like son, Mo told his mother that even when *her* hair turned all gray and she was covered in wrinkles, he would still call her Honeybunch.

So that was one special thing about Mo's family, something that no one else knew about.

But Mo needed more examples for his essay, so he decided to interview his father.

Mo asked his dad how he had met his mom. Mo's dad was always saying that it was the most romantic thing ever, but he'd never told Mo why. Now Mo felt like he was old enough to know how his parents had met, so he asked his dad to tell the story.

"It's a long story—" began Mr. Ma.

"Well, make it short, then," said Mo. He might be old enough for a romantic story, but he had his limits.

"Where should I start?" asked his father.

"Start with how you got to know Honeybunch."

Mo's dad gazed up at the ceiling and smiled. But

Mo didn't like seeing his dad with a corny expression on his face, so he looked away.

"Your mom and I were both students at Art College. I was a junior. One day, one of my roommates was talking about a freshman girl. He said she was the prettiest girl in the whole college. You have no idea how many guys wanted to go out with her—a whole platoon!"

"How many people are in a platoon?" asked Mo.

"How many people are in your class?" said his dad.

"Forty-eight."

"Yes, that's about right. Exactly forty-eight other guys wanted to go out with your mom." Mo's dad continued his story. "No one had any idea how to ask her on a date. But I had a plan. First, I went to a lot of trouble trying to find out what Honeybunch liked. I found out she loved two things: 1) eating and 2) laughing at jokes. This was great news for me, because as you know, I am 1) a great chef and 2) very funny. So I began to cook delicious food every day in the students' kitchen. In the beginning, your mom just ignored me and walked straight past the kitchen to her room. But then the smells from the food I was cooking were just too tempting. She wandered into the kitchen and tried some of the food. She said it was delicious! And the sight of me in a chef's hat and apron made her laugh so much, she was hooked!"

So now Mo had something else to write about. But he still needed more information.

Honeybunch was a window display or showcase designer, which was something very few people in Mo's school knew about. Mo had once told his best friends Hippo, Monkey, and Penguin that his mom was a display designer. They weren't sure what that meant. They thought Mo's mom must design suitcases that were used in movies and plays.

"Mo, what an interesting job your mom has," said Penguin, not looking very convinced. "Uh—designing cases for shows!"

"What is there to design? And what are the cases used for, anyway?" Monkey had even less of an idea about what showcase design meant.

But Mrs. Ma's job had nothing to do with designing luggage. Actually, she designed displays for the store windows of large department stores to attract customers to go inside.

Mo could still remember a time when he was six years old. It was International Children's Day and Honeybunch took Mo to a large shopping mall. Honeybunch was going to display children's clothes in the store window. But there were too many articles of clothing, and she couldn't fit all the mannequins inside the display area.

But Honeybunch wasn't going to let that stop her! Instead of using mannequins, she decided to use real children to model the clothes. She asked Mo and Angel, Mo's neighbor and friend, to be her models for the day. Honeybunch designed the store window as a T-shaped fashion runway. As soon as the curtain for the stage went up, shoppers in the mall could see Mo and Angel standing on the stage wearing brand-new children's clothes. And every time the curtains went down, Mo and Angel changed into other outfits and Honeybunch asked them to pose differently.

Lots of boys and girls crowded around the store window and begged their parents to buy them new clothes when they saw something they really liked. At the end of the day, nearly all the clothing from the display was sold!

Good showcase designers help stores sell their products—and that was just what Honeybunch had done! So she was a really *special* showcase designer.

Now he had enough information to put in his essay.

Ms. Qin was right, Mo thought. *My family really is special!*

A TALENTED SON

Lately, Honeybunch had been making a lot of phone calls, asking about which brand of piano she should purchase.

"Who are you buying a piano for?" Mo asked.

"For you, of course."

Mo was not impressed: he didn't want a piano! "But why didn't you ask me if I wanted a piano?" he said.

"Daisy has a piano."

Daisy was Mo's cousin, the daughter of Honeybunch's sister. Daisy was three months younger than Mo, but she was even *more* mischievous than he was. Honeybunch's sister had tried everything to make Daisy a well-behaved young lady, including making Daisy take ballet lessons, violin lessons, singing lessons, and now . . . piano lessons.

Honeybunch's sister was always persuading Honeybunch that Mo should do the same so that he could become a well-behaved young man! When Daisy started violin lessons, Mo had to start violin lessons as well. But soon after Mo began learning to play the violin, his neck became crooked. Whenever someone asked Mo why his neck was crooked, Mo would blame it on the violin. Honeybunch did want a well-behaved son, but not a well-behaved son with a crooked neck. So Mo stopped taking violin lessons. And Daisy's mother stopped Daisy's violin lessons when she could no longer stand the screeching sound of Daisy trying to play the violin!

But Honeybunch's sister was not someone who gave up easily. After the violin plan failed, she was soon plotting something else. She heard that learning to play traditional instruments could help her daughter get into better schools, so she talked

Honeybunch into sending their kids to learn to play *erhu*[1] together. But Daisy and Mo both hated learning *erhu*, so they decided to make their *erhu* lesson a nightmare for their teacher. The *erhu* teacher was very patient with them, teaching them over and over again the skills they needed to play well. But Daisy and Mo ignored everything the teacher said and played the way they wanted to. The two kids had just three lessons, and the teacher had to end the lesson earlier each time to save himself from the torture of hearing them play. After the third lesson, the teacher simply gave up.

Then Honeybunch's sister heard that children who played the piano were more likely to do well in life, because playing the piano helps to develop quick thinking and willpower. She immediately bought a piano for Daisy . . . and persuaded Honeybunch that she should buy one for Mo.

Honeybunch looked at several pianos and finally bought a shiny black baby grand piano for Mo. Mo was very disappointed—he didn't think it was grand at all! It couldn't even play a beat like an electric keyboard!

[1] A traditional Chinese two-stringed instrument

"Mo, you must try hard to learn to play the piano," said Honeybunch as she tapped the keys of the piano. "This piano was *very* expensive, you know."

"If it was that expensive, then you should just return it," Mo said.

"But why?"

"Because I don't *want* to learn to play the piano."

"But Mo, every child needs to learn something outside school."

"In that case, I'll do martial arts."

There was a sixth grader in Mo's school who did martial arts. He could do moves just like Kung Fu masters. He could jump up in the air, kick a leg out to the side, and no one ever dared to bully him. He was a celebrity in the school and all the boys worshipped him.

But Mo's mother thought her son was mischievous and playful enough as it was. If he learned martial arts, he'd never focus on his schoolwork.

So Honeybunch refused to let Mo learn martial arts.

13

"Mo, your auntie said all children who learn to play the piano will do great things when they grow up."

There was *no way* Mo was going to learn to play the piano. But he could see that it would be a waste if this brand-new piano sat in their living room, unused and taking up loads of space.

Mo had an idea. If he could *sell* the piano, he wouldn't have to take lessons *and* the piano wouldn't go to waste. That would be killing two birds with one stone!

Mo found a piece of paper and wrote down **PIANO FOR SALE**. Then he wrote his phone number underneath and went and stuck the poster on a streetlight outside the block of apartments where he lived.

Shortly afterward, the phone rang. Honeybunch picked it up before Mo could reach it.

"Hello, what make is your piano, please?" asked a strange voice.

"Strauss, imported," replied Mo's mother, thinking it must have been the store she bought it from.

"Which model is it?"

"Model twelve."

"How much do you want to sell it for?"

14

"What? I'm not selling the piano!" said Honeybunch, surprised.

"Not selling? Lady, don't you have better things to do than to advertise something that isn't for sale?"

"Hey, what do you mean? What's going on?" asked Honeybunch, but the person on the other end of the line had already hung up.

"Honeybunch, who was it?" Mo's dad asked.

"I don't know. Someone thought we were selling our piano."

"Don't worry. I'm sure it was just a wrong number," Mo's dad reassured Honeybunch.

But Mo *knew* it wasn't a wrong number!

★

The phone rang again. Mo rushed to the phone and picked it up.

"Hello, how much do you want to sell your piano for?"

Mo vaguely remembered the price of the piano had the number five in it.

"Fifty thousand."

"What? Fifty thousand? Are you out of your mind?"

Mo thought he could picture the person at the other end of the phone.

If the price wasn't fifty thousand, then maybe it was five thousand?

"I mean, five thousand."

"Deal! I'll come over and pick it up right now. Tell me your address."

Mo told the person his address and made sure he got it right.

"Mo, what was that about?" asked Mo's dad suspiciously. "I heard you saying something about fifty thousand and five thousand."

"Oh, it was only Monkey. He's coming to ask me about some math problems."

"Asking *you*?" Mo's dad laughed. "Monkey *must* be having problems!"

Then the front doorbell rang.

Mo rushed to open the door. He saw four very big and strong-looking men standing outside. The men made Mo feel nervous. They looked like four burglars, but without stockings over their heads! Mo wasn't sure it was safe to let them in. . . .

MiDNiGHT
COMMOTiON

"We're here for the piano," said one of the men.

"Is something wrong with it?" asked Honeybunch, coming from the kitchen.

"This guy is the piano tuner," said another of the men. He dragged a short, nervous-looking man from behind the four tough-looking giants. "He wants to make sure that the piano sounds right."

Honeybunch thought there might be something wrong with the new piano and that the piano tuner had come to fix it. She thought Mo's dad must have arranged it. She invited the piano tuner and the rest of the men inside.

The piano tuner took a good look at the piano, lifting up the lid and inspecting the strings. He didn't say a word, but nodded silently to the buyer, one of the giants. Then the tuner sat down in front of the piano, opened the lid, and played an arpeggio. The sound was crystal clear, like a cascading stream. The tuner then played something else. Mo thought that the piano sounded much better than a violin or an *erhu*. What a pity he wasn't able to play it.

"Is there something wrong with the piano?" Honeybunch asked the tuner worriedly.

But the tuner ignored Honeybunch. He nodded again to the buyer.

The buyer took out a wad of cash from his pocket and slammed it on the piano. "I'll take it. Here's five thousand yuan!"

"What? What do you mean 'take it'? Who said anything about selling the piano?"

Honeybunch and Mo's dad were both very confused, but Mo wasn't. As no one was paying attention to him, he snuck away to his own room.

"Didn't you say the piano was for sale?" the buyer said, just as confused as Mo's parents. "You put up an ad, and you told me to come to your place. You agreed to sell it for five thousand. Now my people are here and you're telling me you've changed your mind about selling it?"

"My goodness, only five thousand yuan?" Mo's dad laughed. "We bought that piano two days ago for *thirty-five* thousand. I can't believe its value has decreased by thirty thousand yuan in only two days, ha ha."

Honeybunch remembered the phone call she'd answered. She looked around and couldn't see Mo in the living room. Suddenly, it dawned on her what was happening.

"We are so sorry! *So* sorry! There has been a terrible mistake," Honeybunch said. "But this piano is not for sale, *absolutely* not. My mischievous son has played a trick on all of us."

★

The buyer was mad. But he couldn't stay mad at a child's trick for long. "Okay, okay. No harm done. Let's go then!" But before the buyer and his gang stepped out of the door, he said to Mo's parents, "Make sure you teach that kid a good lesson!"

"We will! We promise!" Mo's parents apologized again.

Mo had done it this time. He was in big trouble.

"Mo, come out of your room this minute!" yelled Honeybunch.

Mo came out of his room and stood in front of Honeybunch with his head down, looking as obedient as he possibly could. He knew a dozen ways to get himself out of trouble.

"Mo, did you put up an ad saying the piano was for sale? And did you tell those people to come over and buy it?"

"Okay, okay, I admit it. But they've gone and the piano is still here. It's all over now," Mo said calmly.

Honeybunch knew Mo was right, but she also knew he had been very bad. She wanted to know, too, why he had tried to sell the piano.

"If it was sold, I wouldn't have to learn to play it," said Mo, as if it were obvious.

But since Mo's plan to sell the piano had failed, he would have to learn to play the piano.

From that day on, Honeybunch stopped attending her aerobics class and stayed at home every night watching Mo practicing the piano.

Mo was really suffering. He hated practicing. And he hated having piano lessons. How could he persuade his mother to let him stop? He'd managed to stop taking violin lessons and *erhu* lessons. He *must* stop taking piano lessons.

Very soon Mo came up with an idea!

★

It was midnight. The alarm clock in Mo's room woke him up right on time. Mo quickly got out of bed.

He went to the living room and began playing the piano.

The sound of him playing was as horrible as you could imagine, and it was loud enough for all the neighbors to hear.

"Mo, are you out of your mind?" said Honeybunch. She was standing in the doorway to the living room, looking sleepy and rumpled.

"Nope, I am not out of my mind. I want to play the piano! I *love* playing the piano! I'm going to play all night long." Mo pounded the piano keys with his fists.

There was a pounding at the front door. "Who's playing the piano at this hour? We're trying to sleep!" yelled the neighbors.

Honeybunch was desperate. "Mo, stop it at once. I'm begging you!"

"No, I'm going to play every day, and I will play at midnight, too!"

Honeybunch knew it was hopeless. When it came to her only child, she couldn't stay mad for long. She gave in. "All right, Mo, you win. I will *never, never* ask you to play the piano again!"

"It's a deal!" Mo hooked his pinky with his mom's pinky and said, "Little fingers intertwined; a promise can't be undermined; it must stay true till the end of time!"

Mo went back to bed feeling great.

But Honeybunch couldn't sleep. Why oh why was her son so mischievous?

"I was even worse when I was Mo's age!" Mo's dad said to comfort her. "But look how great I turned out."

He was right. And who knew? Maybe one day Mo would become a successful man, like his dad. But then again, maybe he wouldn't!

MEN'S TALK

It was almost the weekend.

Ms. Qin said to the class, "Don't forget, Sunday is Mother's Day. You should all plan to give your mothers a meaningful and unforgettable day. In fact, your homework for the weekend is to write an essay called 'An Unforgettable Mother's Day.'"

Ms. Qin never let her class have a weekend without homework, and Mother's Day weekend was no exception.

As usual, Mo had to ask a question. "Ms. Qin, what do you mean by an 'Unforgettable Mother's Day'?"

"That's for you to figure out! You should talk about it with your father, and ask him to think of something."

★

At the dinner table the next night, Mo said, "Dad, there's something I need to talk to you about."

"Sure," Mo's dad replied. "Go ahead, ask."

"Not now."

"Why not?"

"Because it's men's talk. We can't let Mom hear it."

Honeybunch laughed so hard she almost choked on her food. "Mo, since when did you become a man?"

"Of course I'm a man," Mo said. "I was born a man."

After dinner, Mo asked his dad if they could go for a walk to discuss private matters.

"Where shall we walk?"

"If you needed to talk business with another man, where would you go?" Mo asked.

"A restaurant?"

Mo shook his head. "We've already had dinner."

"A teahouse?"

Mo shook his head again. "I don't drink tea."

"A coffee shop?"

"Does it sell ice cream?"

"I guess so."

So Mo and his dad went to a coffee shop. Mo's dad ordered an espresso. Mo ordered an ice-cream sundae with fresh fruit and a little umbrella for decoration.

"Mo, what is it you want to talk to me about?"

"Do you know what day tomorrow is?"

"Tomorrow?"

Mo's dad thought for a long time, but he couldn't think of anything special about the next day.

"Tomorrow is Mother's Day."

"Are you serious?!" Mo's dad said, panicking. "Thank goodness you mentioned it! I was going to spend the whole day tomorrow watching the World Cup. I can't do that now. I'll have to go to your grandmother's house and celebrate Mother's Day with her. Mo, you can come with me."

"But what about Honeybunch?" Mo said. "I have to celebrate Mother's Day with *my* mom, not yours."

"You're right," said Mo's dad. "You will spend Mother's Day with your mom, and I will spend it with my mom. Now, before the stores close, I must buy a present for my mom."

"What about me?!" Mo said, pulling his dad back. "How should I spend Mother's Day with *my* mom tomorrow? That's what I wanted to talk to you about."

"However you want to spend it."

"But Ms. Qin said it has to be meaningful and unforgettable."

"As long as you spend Mother's Day with Honeybunch, she'll think it's meaningful. And I'm sure she'll think it's unforgettable. What do you think?"

Mo thought what his dad said made sense.

Mr. Ma couldn't wait to get to the stores before they closed. He took out three hundred yuan from his wallet and handed it to Mo.

"Mo, this is for Mother's Day."

"No, thanks, Dad, I don't want it. I have my own money."

Mo decided that he had to use his own money since it would be *him* who was planning Mother's Day. Mo had some money that he'd gotten from his parents for his last birthday saved in the bank. Mo was determined to give Honeybunch the best Mother's Day ever. No amount of money would be too much for that.

Mo had already made up his mind about what they'd do for Mother's Day: it would be a full day of nonstop fun activities! Mo thought of all the things he wanted to do with Honeybunch.

After Mo got back home, Honeybunch nagged him to tell her what he and his father had discussed.

"It was men's talk," Mo said.

But Honeybunch was a very curious person. And when anyone tried to keep something from her, it only made her more curious!

"But Mo, I'm your mother. Why can't you tell me about it even if it is a men's thing?"

"But Mom, I can't tell you because you're a woman."

"If you tell me, I'll let you have some ice cream."

Normally, Honeybunch wouldn't let Mo eat ice cream at night. But Mo had already eaten a large ice-cream sundae in the coffee shop, so Honeybunch's bribe didn't work.

"I don't want it, thank you," Mo said, going back to his room. "I'm going to do my homework."

Mo shut the door to his room. But he didn't do his homework. Instead, he started drawing. He drew a little brood of chicks around a hen. There was a ribbon around the hen's neck and Mo wrote on it, *Happy Mother's Day!* Then he wrote underneath the drawing, *To Honeybunch; from Mo!*

MOTHER'S DAY OR MO'S DAY?

Honeybunch never slept late, not even on the weekend. She liked to get up early in the morning to make breakfast—three different breakfasts for three different people. Mo's breakfast was always oatmeal with milk, his dad's breakfast was rice crispies with rich soybean milk, and Honeybunch liked fruit salad.

Honeybunch got up, went into the kitchen, and walked over to the fridge. When she saw what was stuck on the fridge door, tears came to her eyes. Her dear boy, Mo, had drawn a picture just for her and written a Mother's Day message on it!

She was still looking at the picture when Mo walked into the kitchen wearing his slippers. She suddenly remembered she was supposed to be making breakfast.

"Mom, you don't need to make breakfast today. We're going out for breakfast," said Mo, sounding very grown-up. "Today, I'm taking you out for an unforgettable Mother's Day!"

★

When they were dressed, Mo took his mom out. Honeybunch didn't even ask where they were going.

Mo wanted to go to the cash machine to get some money, but Honeybunch said she had money on her.

"We can't use your money!" Mo said. "Today is Mother's Day, so of course all *expenses* will be on me." He'd heard his father say this to some of his clients, and Mo thought his mother would be impressed to hear him behaving in such an adult manner.

Mo took out three hundred yuan from the cash machine. With so much cash on him, Mo felt like a real big shot.

Honeybunch and Mo walked by several cafés that were serving breakfast, but Mo passed them without even looking at them. Finally, they came to a fried chicken restaurant. Mo stopped and asked Honeybunch, "What would you like for breakfast?"

"Um . . ." What Honeybunch really wanted was fruit salad.

"Name anything you want." Mo felt the wad of cash in his pocket. "I'm rich!"

"I want to eat fried chicken."

Instead of saying what *she* really wanted to eat, Honeybunch said what she knew *Mo* wanted to eat.

"Great. Fried chicken it is."

It was still early. There wasn't a single customer in the fried chicken restaurant. Mo and Honeybunch were the first customers of the day. They were served like royalty!

"Honeybunch, name anything you want to eat." Mo felt the wad of cash in his pocket. "I'm rich!"

Honeybunch only ordered lemon tea. Mo ordered lots of food: a spicy chicken sandwich, an order of small fries, a chocolate milkshake, and an extra large ice-cold cola.

After breakfast, Mo suggested to Honeybunch that they go shopping in the pedestrian-only shopping street.

That was exactly what Honeybunch wanted to do.

The pedestrian shopping street was lined with stores on both sides. But Honeybunch didn't care what the stores were selling, only what they *looked* like. She wanted to check out all the displays in the store windows.

Honeybunch designed store windows for some of the largest stores on the shopping street. Their store windows looked extravagant and spectacular. But Honeybunch paid special attention to the store windows of retail stores selling designer brands. Although their windows weren't big, they were unique and special in their own ways. If it had been any other day, Mo would have lost his patience when Honeybunch spent so much time looking at store windows. But on this particular day, Mo was prepared to put up with it. He said to Honeybunch, "No problem, take as much time as you like."

Then it was time for lunch. Mo and Honeybunch passed many Chinese restaurants, western-style restaurants, and hot-pot restaurants, and finally stopped in front of a pizzeria.

"Honeybunch, what do you want for lunch?"

What Honeybunch really wanted was a hot pot with lots of mushrooms, but instead she said, "I want pizza for lunch."

"No problem," said Mo, as that was just what *he* wanted.

Mo ordered a medium-size pizza for the two of them. But Honeybunch couldn't even finish one slice.

After they'd left the pizzeria, Mo asked Honeybunch, "Where else would you like to go?"

Honeybunch wanted to spend more time looking at store windows, but instead she told Mo she wanted to go to the amusement park, since she knew that was what he wanted to do!

Mo agreed eagerly. "Of course, since today is Mother's Day, we must go to the amusement park!"

Mo had a great time at the amusement park. Mo's favorite ride was the roller coaster. It was SO exciting.

"Honeybunch, let's go on the roller coaster together."

Mo dragged Honeybunch to the roller coaster, which she knew she was going to hate. She felt sick right after, and she had to sit on the bench at the amusement park for the rest of the afternoon.

It was getting dark and Honeybunch was feeling much better. Mo tried every ride in the park and finally came back to meet Honeybunch on the bench.

After they left the amusement park, Mo immediately spotted a McDonald's.

"Honeybunch, what do you want for dinner?"

What Honeybunch *really* wanted was to have a simple meal at home, but she still picked what she knew Mo wanted.

"Let's go to McDonald's for dinner."

Honeybunch didn't order anything at McDonald's. Mo felt very sorry for her. He felt in his pocket and found he still had some money left. He decided he should buy a beautiful Mother's Day present for Honeybunch.

"Honeybunch, what present do you want? Name anything you want, and I'll buy it for you."

Honeybunch tried very hard to stifle a giggle. She didn't want to hurt Mo's feelings. He was trying to be so grown-up.

Honeybunch saw a store on the other side of the road that sold hair decorations. She told Mo she wanted to buy a hair comb.

Honeybunch saw a hair comb in the shape of the star sign Pisces. She liked it at once because her star sign was Pisces.

"How much is this hair comb?" she inquired.

"Thirty yuan."

"That's too expensive," said Honeybunch.

"Buy it if you like it," said Mo, trying to sound like a man. "Miss, I'll take that hair comb. Please wrap it for me."

Mo only had two coins left after he'd paid the thirty yuan. He thought the day had been a huge success. Mo had spent all his money, and he could now write his essay for Ms. Qin. And this is what he wrote:

An Unforgettable Mother's Day

In the morning, I took my mother to eat fried chicken.
Before lunch, I took my mother shopping.
For lunch, I took my mother to eat pizza.
In the afternoon, we went to the amusement park.
For dinner, we ate at McDonald's.

Mo didn't write anything about what his mother

thought was the single most important and nicest moment of the day—that Mo had bought her a hair comb.

It wasn't because Mo had forgotten about giving his mother the hair comb; it was simply because Mo wasn't *interested* in it. Mo was much more interested in fried chicken, pizza, and the amusement park!

When Ms. Qin marked Mo's essay, she wrote at the end of the page, "Was it a special day for your mother, or for you?"

PAID HOUSEWORK

The next time Honeybunch came back from her sister's house, she said she wanted to talk to Mo about something really important.

"What's the matter?" said Mo, lounging on the sofa. "Did Auntie come up with another one of her stupid ideas?"

Mo didn't really like his auntie. Though he did like his cousin because she was even more mischievous than him! But instead of disciplining her own daughter, Mo's auntie seemed very fond of sharing her ideas for disciplining Mo. . . .

"Mo, your auntie has heard from your uncle that in America parents pay their kids to do chores around the house. And now your auntie pays your cousin Daisy to do chores."

"Aha," said Mo, suddenly interested. He liked the sound of being paid. . . .

Mo's mother continued. "Daisy gets paid ten cents per room for vacuuming; ten cents for watering the flowers; ten cents for washing the dishes. For doing the laundry, she gets ten cents for every article of clothing."

Ten cents . . . ten cents . . . and another ten cents . . . Mo began to imagine his pockets bulging with money.

Mo had to agree that getting paid to do chores wasn't such a bad idea at all. Mo had always done some chores, but he'd never thought of asking his parents to pay him for them before. What a brilliant idea!

Mo would be a fool not to take the money. He decided to take immediate action and earn as much money as he could.

First Mo got the vacuum cleaner from the closet. He vacuumed the living room, then the dining room, the study, his bedroom, and finally his parents' bedroom.

Mo's dad was sleeping. He had worked all last night finishing off a design project. Just as he was falling asleep, the sound of the vacuum cleaner woke him up.

"Mo, for goodness' sake. Why are you vacuuming? I'm trying to sleep."

But making money was much more important to Mo than sleeping.

Mo ignored his father and went on vacuuming.

Mo's father hated it when he couldn't get his sleep. "Mo, please let me sleep!"

"But I want to make money!" Mo said. "Honeybunch said I can earn ten cents for every room I vacuum."

"Here, take this!" Mo's dad got out of bed and pulled out a ten yuan note from his wallet and smacked it on the bedside table. "Now stop vacuuming at once!"

Brilliant! Mo had earned ten whole yuan for vacuuming the bedroom alone. He did a somersault on the sofa!

Now that he'd discovered he could make money by doing household chores, Mo was on a roll. He vacuumed three more rooms nonstop. He didn't feel tired at all, so he figured he would do even more chores.

Mo took out every bowl, plate, and dish from the kitchen cabinets. He counted how many there were as he washed them. There was a total of thirty pieces, which meant he could earn another three yuan by washing bowls, plates, and dishes alone.

Suddenly there was a *crash*. A plate slipped from Mo's hand and broke into smithereens.

"Mo, *please,* could you just let me sleep?!" yelled Mo's dad as he charged into the kitchen.

"What are you doing washing all those bowls?" he asked curiously.

"Mom said I can earn ten cents for every bowl I wash," replied Mo.

"But those bowls are already clean. There's no need to wash them. Besides, you broke one. Ha, you will have to pay for that."

"How much?"

"About twelve yuan."

Poor Mo. That was about everything he had earned that morning. It wasn't fair!

But Mo wasn't someone who gave up easily. He decided to start from scratch again and earn more money. Mo had another idea!

Honeybunch said Mo could earn ten cents for washing one piece of clothing. Mo knew just how he could earn lots of money.

Mo dashed into his parents' bedroom and woke up his dad again.

"Mo, this is getting ridiculous. PLEASE let me get some sleep."

"In a minute, Dad. I want some clothes to wash!"

Mo's dad sat up and said, "In that case, why don't you wash my socks?"

"How much?"

"Ten cents per pair."

"But your socks stink. I'll wash them, but I'll charge ten cents for each sock."

"All right, all right, ten cents per sock then. NOW LET ME GET SOME SLEEP."

Both Mo and his dad had super-stinky feet. Usually, Honeybunch did the laundry. But Mo's dad never let her wash his stinky socks. He hid all his socks in a place only he knew about. When he had only one pair of clean socks left, he would wash all his dirty socks himself.

Mo's dad took out six pairs of stinky socks. Mo counted twelve socks, which meant he could earn 120 cents—that's one yuan and twenty cents. Not much! Mo saw another pair of socks on the nightstand, and was about to grab them as well.

"Not those," yelled his dad. "I need those for tonight's party."

But Mo didn't care about his dad's party. He had only one thing on his mind, and that was to make more money. Washing an extra pair of socks meant he could earn another twenty cents. Seeing his dad put his head on the pillow again, Mo grabbed the clean pair of socks and put them together with the dirty socks. He also grabbed Honeybunch's lovely soft wool sweater, which was on the chair. Mo threw everything into the washing machine together.

Washing machines are so EASY. Mo could earn loads of money without even having to put his hands in soapy water.

★

An hour later, Mo's dad woke up and roared like a lion. "WHERE ARE MY SOCKS?!"

"It's okay, Dad, they're in the washing machine."

"I don't believe it," Mo's dad fell back onto the bed and cried loudly. "What do I do now? That was my last pair of clean socks!"

"The washing machine will be done in a second," Mo said.

Mo's dad was already mad to begin with, and now he was even madder. "I'd rather go to the party with bare feet than wear wet socks!"

"Then go with bare feet," Mo replied. "Bare feet are cool! You could also shave your head. Then everyone will stare at your head instead of your feet."

Mo's dad didn't know whether to laugh or cry. "Mo, what am I going to do with you?"

Just then, Honeybunch came back from the hair salon and started getting ready to go to the dinner party with Mo's dad.

"Where's my lovely soft wool sweater that was on the bedroom chair?" she cried.

"In the washing machine. I thought you'd like it to be really clean for the party. It's just spin-drying now!" Mo told his mom happily.

"Waa! Waa! Waa!" wailed Honeybunch.

Mo was stunned. He had never heard his mother make such a noise. He had washed her sweater; she should be pleased.

Mo's dad immediately opened the washing machine and took out the beautiful soft wool sweater. But it was much too late; the damage was done. The sweater had shrunk—it wasn't wearable, except by a doll. Mo was in trouble again!

Mo was fed up. He had spent the whole day doing housework and he hadn't earned one cent. He had even had to give up his savings so that his mother could buy a new sweater. And worse, both his parents were really, really mad at him. What was a boy supposed to do?

CRYSTAL SLIPPERS

Luckily for Mo, the next weekend's homework assignment meant he could make up for the mess he'd made of doing the laundry. Because Ms. Qin said that over the weekend, everyone had to do something to show they cared for their parents. Then they had to write about it as a homework essay.

As usual, Mo had to ask Ms. Qin a question. "What kind of thing would show we care for our parents?"

"Well, Mo, you could cook a meal for them, or you could wash their feet; and—"

Mo liked the idea of washing his parents' feet, even

though his dad's feet stank. But it could be fun! Although Ms. Qin went on and gave lots more examples, Mo had already decided that the "something" he was going to do was to wash his parents' feet, whether they liked it or not.

★

As soon as Mo got home, he announced to his parents that he was going to make up for the laundry fiasco and do something to show he really cared for them.

"Great!" said his dad. "I was just thinking about a back massage!"

Mo's father lay on the floor and waited for Mo to start the massage.

But Mo said, "Get up, please, Dad. Ms. Qin said we should offer to wash our parents' feet; she didn't say anything about a back massage."

"Great! I was just thinking about washing my feet!" Mo's dad quickly got up and took off his shoes and socks.

PHEW! Mo held his breath and acted as if he was about to pass out. "Give me a break. I don't want to suffocate from your stinky feet. I think I'll wash Mom's feet instead."

Mo asked Honeybunch to sit on the sofa. Honeybunch was so touched when she heard Mo was going to wash her feet. She even had tears in her eyes.

Mo got a bowl from the kitchen. But as soon as he placed Honeybunch's feet in the basin, his dad yelled, "That bowl is for washing vegetables. You can't use it for washing feet!"

Normally, Mo's dad wouldn't make such a big fuss over such a little thing. Mo thought his dad was jealous that he wasn't having his feet washed by his precious son!

Mo got out a different bowl from the bathroom and placed Honeybunch's feet in it. Then he ran to his room and wrote down what he had just done, in case he forgot when it came to writing his essay.

It was a very cold day, and Honeybunch had her bare feet in the basin. She couldn't quite understand why Mo had just disappeared.

"Mo!" shouted his dad. "Do you want your mother's feet to freeze?!"

Mo came back holding a kettle. The kettle was filled with boiling water, and Mo was just about to pour it right into the bowl. Fortunately, his dad was quick enough to stop him.

"Mo, what are you doing? Do you want your mother's feet to burn?!"

Mo knew that his father was just acting jealous: yelling one second that Mo wanted to freeze Honeybunch's feet, and the next that he wanted to burn them.

"Don't just stand there, Mo," said his dad. "Go and get some cold water from the kitchen," he ordered.

Mo fetched a jug of cold water, put it next to Honeybunch's feet, and ran back to his room to write this step down in case he forgot.

When Mo reappeared from his room, he found his dad washing Honeybunch's feet. Honeybunch had her eyes closed and looked totally relaxed. She was enjoying every second of having her feet washed. She was even humming a little tune.

"Stop!" Mo yelled. "Ms. Qin assigned this homework to *me*, not *you*!"

Honeybunch opened her eyes and realized it was her husband who was washing her feet. She had thought it was Mo, which was why she was enjoying it so much.

"You?" Honeybunch glared at her husband. "It is

our son who wanted to wash my feet, not you!"

Poor Mr. Ma—now *he* couldn't seem to get anything right.

It was a victory for Mo. He happily shoved his dad aside.

Mo carefully massaged Honeybunch's feet as he washed them. Honeybunch's toenails had silver nail polish on them; they looked really pretty. Mo began to think about a pair of crystal slippers in a fairy tale he had once read. Honeybunch's feet were so pretty, he thought she deserved a pair of crystal slippers.

"Mo, what are you thinking about?" asked his mom.

"When I'm grown-up, I'll buy you a pair of crystal slippers," he said.

"Mo, that's so sweet. What a good boy you are. I'll remember what you just said as long as I live."

Mo ran back to his room again because he wanted to write down what his mom had just said. Meanwhile, Honeybunch began dreaming about her pair of crystal slippers. She dreamed of wearing the pair of slippers her lovely, courteous, *well-behaved* son had just bought her, and dancing with a charming, grown-up Mo in a fairy-tale ballroom.

But as Honeybunch dreamed on, the water in the

bowl became cold, and soon her feet began to freeze—this wasn't part of the fairy tale.

After Mo had finished scribbling in his notebook, he ran back and saw that the water was no longer hot. He picked up the kettle and poured the not-quite-boiling water into the bowl without thinking twice.

"Aaaaaaah!" Honeybunch screamed.

Mo panicked and threw the kettle on the floor. The lid came off, and the floor was soaked with water.

"What's going on?" Mo's dad shouted, running out of his study.

Mo was so shocked that he stood there completely still.

Honeybunch was shocked too. One minute ago, she was dreaming about her pretty feet wearing crystal slippers, and now her pretty feet were red and swollen. There was no way they would even *fit* into a pair of crystal slippers.

Mo was miserable. He hated seeing his mother hurt. He hated himself for deciding that he would wash Honeybunch's feet. If he had given his father a back massage, he was sure everything would have been all right.

Mo had never felt so upset in his entire life. But he didn't want to cry; crying was for babies, not for precious sons.

"Mo," said his dad. "If you want to cry, don't hold it back."

"Don't worry, sweetheart!" Honeybunch hugged Mo and said, "Mommy is really happy today because

 55

you did something that showed you really cared for her!"

Mo looked at his mom's pretty feet. Her pretty feet should be wearing crystal slippers, but now they were about to be wrapped in bandages.

Mo finally began to cry—it was SO hard to be a good son and to have fun too!

TWELVE-LAYER SANDWICH

For the first time ever, Mo's essay got a really good grade—ninety out of one hundred. Ms. Qin read it out loud to the whole class. After she'd finished she asked the students why they thought she had given Mo such a high grade on his essay.

"Because Mo wrote down every step, and every step was written very clearly," Monkey said loyally.

Mo lowered his head. He knew that he hadn't written down everything that had happened. He didn't write down the bit about scalding his mother's feet.

Then Lily said, "The essay was really imaginative too. Also, you could really tell what the writer was feeling as he washed his mother's feet."

The essay made Ms. Qin change her opinion of Mo just a little. If he was able to write such an essay, it proved that he was a loving and kind child, and that he loved his mother very much.

After school, Ms. Qin asked Mo to go to her office. Ms. Qin quite often asked Mo to go to her office, usually to scold him. But not this time. Ms. Qin didn't scold Mo; instead, she smiled at him. Mo had become so used to Ms. Qin yelling at him that he wasn't quite sure how to react to her smile. He felt rather shy.

Ms. Qin saw Mo was embarrassed, but she wanted to tell him something.

"Mo, I could tell from your essay that you care for your parents very much. But caring for your parents for just a day or two is far from being good enough. You have to show you care for the rest of your life. Can you do this?"

Mo was determined that he would. He would carry on doing things to show he cared, especially for his mom. But he didn't dare offer to wash her feet again!

Then Mo had an idea. He remembered Ms. Qin saying that cooking a meal for your parents was another good way to show you care for them.

Mo decided to cook a meal for his mother.

Mo always liked to do things differently from other people. He decided to cook something for Honeybunch that she wouldn't have seen before—something she'd never forget.

There was a huge fridge in the kitchen that was always crammed with a variety of food—cheese, meat, vegetables, fruit . . . even chocolate!

Mo had already made up his mind about what he was going to make. He took out a sliced loaf of bread from the fridge, then took out Honeybunch's favorite blue and red striped plate from the dishwasher. Mo decided to make Honeybunch a twelve-layer sandwich!

Layer one: mango slices
Layer two: cold roast beef
Layer three: tomato slices

Layer four: chicken drumstick
Layer five: peanut butter
Layer six: strawberry sauce
Layer seven: five-spice fish slices
Layer eight: banana slices
Layer nine: cucumber slices
Layer ten: kiwi fruit slices
Layer eleven: lettuce

And on the twelfth layer—the top layer—Mo squeezed out some mayonnaise and made it into a pyramid shape. Then the crowning glory—he decorated the tip of the pyramid with a red cherry.

The twelve-layer sandwich was almost half a meter tall. It looked so colorful and SO mouthwatering. No one could possibly have seen or tried a sandwich like it before, not even the President of the United States or the Queen of England. Certainly not his parents.

This was Mo's masterpiece. The more he looked at it, the more he loved his work.

Mo carefully carried his masterpiece from the kitchen into the living room. On the dining table was a bouquet of red roses in a vase. Mo cut the roses from their stems and placed them on the sandwich plate around the twelve-layer sandwich.

With the roses, this extraordinary sandwich looked even more extraordinary.

As soon as Honeybunch came back from work, she saw the extraordinary sandwich on the dining table.

"Wow, what a magnificent sandwich!" Honeybunch reacted like a surprised little girl. "Mo, have you invited the girls in your class over for tea?"

The only time Mo's mom had seen him make tea before was when Lily and Man Man had come to the apartment.

"No, this is just for you, Mom."

Mo carefully lifted the plate with the twelve-layer sandwich on it and presented it to Honeybunch.

Honeybunch was really touched that Mo had made this magnificent sandwich for her. Mo couldn't understand why. Honeybunch had done so much for Mo, and now all he'd done was make her one sandwich, and she acted like it was a big deal!

"Mom, hurry up and try the sandwich. I want to know what it tastes like."

But the sandwich was so big that Honeybunch didn't know how to take the first bite.

"I am *not* going to eat it," Honeybunch said. "I will save it and ask everyone to come and see what my precious son has made for me!"

There was a large display case in the living room, which was filled with trophies and awards that Mo's father had won. Mr. Ma was a well-known toy designer. His designs had won him lots of awards, especially the one called "Jumping Baby"—inspired by Mo when he was little and liked to jump all the time. That one had won first prize at the international toy fair. The award—a tall gold trophy—was kept in an elegant glass case specially made to display it.

Honeybunch removed the gold cup from the glass case and replaced it with the twelve-layer sandwich that Mo had made for her. The sandwich fit perfectly. It was as if the display case had been made for it.

Honeybunch then moved the glass case to a place in the living room where no one could miss it. Mo's dad saw it right away when he came home from work.

"What's going on? Where's my gold trophy?" Mo's father saw that his priceless gold trophy had been removed from its case. He immediately assumed that Mo was behind it.

"Mo!" Mr. Ma sounded furious.

"Stop putting on that scary face," said Mo's mother. "Our son made me that sandwich. I put it in the glass case, he didn't."

"But which is more important—that sandwich or my gold trophy?!"

"The sandwich, of course," Honeybunch said firmly, "because it was my son who made it for me."

Mo's father thought this was ridiculous. "If it was *our* son who made it for *you*, why don't *you* eat it? Why does it have to be displayed in my glass case?"

"I'm never going to eat it," said Honeybunch. "I want to just look at it every day."

"Hmmmm," replied Mo's father. "I think the problem is, you don't know how to eat such a big sandwich." Mr. Ma burst out laughing when he saw how big the twelve-layer sandwich was. "You'd need the mouth of a hippopotamus or a crocodile to eat that sandwich."

He was right; only someone with a super-big mouth like a hippo or a crocodile could take a bite out of such an enormous sandwich.

But Honeybunch didn't care. Day after day, she

brought friends home to see the twelve-layer sandwich her son had made for her. For quite some time, Honeybunch was the happiest mom in the whole world!

FOOTPRINTS AND FINGERPRINTS

There were two things Honeybunch really loved eating and they were both really strong-smelling foods: the stinkiest stinky tofu and the stinkiest durian fruit. Mo could never understand why Honeybunch loved eating things that were so stinky. He could never understand how she managed to swallow them.

Honeybunch liked to fry the stinky tofu in a pan until it turned golden yellow, and then put it on a plate with red pepper sauce on the side. The stinky tofu was then dipped in the red pepper sauce before eating it. Honeybunch said the taste was simply DIVINE. Mo thought it was disgusting!

Honeybunch knew how much Mo and his dad hated stinky tofu, but she loved it so much that whenever she got a craving to eat stinky tofu, not even her beloved son and husband could stop her.

Mo's father held his nose so that he couldn't smell it and begged Honeybunch, "Honeybunch, please, could you stop eating stinky tofu?"

But Honeybunch was in heaven. She said to her husband, "I can give up any other kind of food, but not stinky tofu!"

Mo pinched his nose too. "I will not eat stinky tofu! I will never eat stinky tofu in my entire life!"

Honeybunch shook her head as she continued to enjoy the stinky tofu. "Mo, if you can't even try stinky tofu, you can't be my son! Maybe they switched babies by accident at the hospital."

Mo wouldn't care if people told him he wasn't like his father, but telling him he wasn't like his mother was a different story.

"I am so your son!"

Honeybunch laughed. "If you are *so* my son, try a bite of stinky tofu!"

Honeybunch picked up a piece of tofu with her chopsticks and pushed it toward Mo. Mo covered his mouth and wouldn't open it one little bit. He'd rather not be Honeybunch's son than eat stinky tofu.

Honeybunch always ate fruit after dinner. Mo's house was always full of fruit, like mangoes, bananas, and apples. But instead of eating *nice* fruit, Honeybunch preferred to eat a fruit called a durian.

Now, a durian is one hundred times stinkier than stinky tofu. It is a strangely shaped tropical fruit about the size of a basketball with a very hard shell. Once you crack open the shell, the flesh inside is soft and milky-colored. The durian is so big that it's impossible to finish a whole one right away. Every time Honeybunch felt like eating a durian, she took a couple of bites, then put the rest back in the fridge.

So not only did Mo and his dad have to hold their

breath during dinner, they also had to hold their breath when they opened the fridge. To make matters worse, everything that came out of the fridge smelled like durian.

"Dad, let's throw Honeybunch's durian away," Mo said one day.

"Throw it away? Where could we throw it?" his dad asked. "Don't forget, your mom reads detective novels every day. She'll find out where we've thrown it sooner or later."

"We could flush it down the toilet. There won't be any trace left of it," Mo suggested.

"I wouldn't dare do that. You can count me out!" Mo's dad refused to throw his wife's favorite fruit away.

Well, you can count me in! Mo thought.

Mo was determined to get rid of the smelly fruit from the fridge, but he couldn't let Honeybunch find out. There were only three people in the family, so if it wasn't his father, it had to be him. You didn't have to be much of a detective to figure out who the culprit was.

Mo had an idea. He would get rid of the fruit in such a way that his mom would think his dad had done it!

Mo waited until his parents had gone to their bedroom. He then got a pair of his father's shoes from the closet, making sure that the shoes he picked had mud on them.

Mo walked toward the fridge in his father's muddy shoes. He looked back to make sure he'd left footprints every step of the way.

There were lots of muddy footprints on the floor, and it was pretty obvious that they were a man's footprints, not a young boy's.

"Ha! You'll be in trouble, Dad. You'll have no place to hide!" Mo giggled.

Mo took out the plate of smelly durian from the fridge, threw it into the toilet, and flushed it.

Flush! Flush! Flush!

The water was swirling around, but the durian was still there because it was too big.

Flush! Flush! Flush!

Mo kept on flushing the toilet until finally the durian was all gone.

Ha! Ha!

Mo took a deep breath. He no longer had to smell the disgusting stinky smell of durian.

The next day, Mo pretended that nothing had

happened. He couldn't wait for Honeybunch to find out.

"Where is my durian?" Honeybunch said, searching the fridge for her leftover durian.

Mo's father pretended to read the newspaper, but gave Mo a suspicious glance. He knew Mo must have gotten rid of the durian, because he knew that *he* hadn't.

"Where is the durian I put in the fridge?" Honeybunch looked at Mo and then at her husband. "Which one of you has hidden it? Wait till I find out."

Honeybunch had been reading lots of detective novels, so she was ready to solve . . . *The Case of the Vanishing Durian.*

Mo couldn't stay silent. He decided to protest his innocence right away. "I never even opened the fridge. Look at all those footprints next to the fridge— it's *obvious* who the guilty person is!"

Mo's mother saw the man-size footprints near the fridge.

"That's impossible!" said Mo's father. "I didn't open the fridge!"

"But there's hard evidence. Don't think you can get away with it this time." Mo smiled triumphantly.

But Honeybunch wasn't paying attention to the

footprints. Instead, she was looking closely at the fingerprints on the fridge door.

"Mo, who do *you* think these fingerprints belong to?" she asked.

On the door of the fridge were three clear fingerprints, all of them child-size!

Mo's father was saved. He put his fingers over the fingerprints on the fridge door. His fingers were SO much bigger!

The fingerprints were hard evidence against Mo. But Mo was going to give it one last try. He walked over the footprints in his own shoes—his footprints were SO much smaller!

But there was no fooling Honeybunch. "Mo, you left those footprints wearing your father's shoes. I knew from the start that it was you. First, you had the *motive*, because you hate the smell of durian. You wanted to make the durian vanish in the toilet, but you didn't want other people to find out that it was you, so you framed your dad. You wore your dad's shoes and left those footprints on purpose, but you forgot about the fingerprints you left on the fridge door. Last night, I heard the sound of the toilet flushing over and over again. At the time, your dad was with me in the bedroom. He was *not* at the scene of the crime, so the one and only criminal in *The Case of the Vanishing Durian* was you, Mo."

Mo was speechless. He had no choice but to admit to his crime. His mother had solved the case, his father had been proven innocent, and Mo, once more, was in trouble!

THE PRETTIEST MOM CONTEST

Mo and Penguin were having an argument.

Penguin said his mom was the prettiest mom in the whole world. Mo disagreed and said *his* mom was the prettiest mom in the whole world.

Penguin was getting madder and madder. "What have you got to prove that your mom is the prettiest in the whole world?"

Mo was also getting angrier and angrier. "What have *you* got to prove that *your* mom is the prettiest

in the whole world?"

"Monkey could prove it. Hippo could prove it. Lily could prove it. Even Man Man could prove it. In fact, all our classmates could prove that my mom is the prettiest in the whole wide world," yelled Penguin.

Monkey, Hippo, and Mo had *all* seen Penguin's mom before. They'd all visited Penguin's house many times, and Penguin's mom always gave them lots of delicious snacks. Their other classmates had seen Penguin's mom, too, because she often came to school to pick up Penguin in her red Porsche—no one could miss her!

"Monkey! Hippo! Tell Mo that my mom is the prettiest mom in the whole world!"

Monkey and Hippo enjoyed watching the fight between Penguin and Mo, but they were completely caught off guard. They felt bad if they didn't agree with Penguin since Penguin's mom gave them treats whenever they went to Penguin's house, but they didn't want to offend Mo, either. They'd never seen Mo's mom, but they thought she was probably quite pretty because Mo said she was, and although he was mischievous, he very rarely lied.

"Yes, yes, she's pretty!" they said without saying which mom they were talking about. . . .

But Penguin wanted to be sure. "Don't play tricks on me now. Who are you saying is pretty?"

"*Penguin's mom* is pretty."

Penguin looked smug. He was definitely going to win the argument. He looked at Mo and asked, "Who can prove that your mom is the prettiest mom in the whole world?"

Mo couldn't think of anyone to prove it. Honeybunch had never come to school, because she was afraid that if she did, Ms. Qin would lecture her about having such a troublemaker for a son.

"If you cannot find anyone to prove it, you must admit that my mom is the prettiest mom in the whole world," said Penguin bossily.

Penguin looked so arrogant with his penguinlike round stomach sticking out of the bottom of his shirt. Mo clenched his fists very tight and tried to hold himself back from hitting Penguin right in the middle of his stomach.

At that moment, Angel turned up and said *she*

could prove that Mo's mom was the prettiest mom in the world.

"I see Mo's mom every day. Her hair is really long, and she uses a fruit-colored lipstick."

What was Angel talking about? Not only did the boys not understand what "fruit-colored" lipstick was, the girls were baffled too.

"You know, that pink-colored lipstick that's kind of glossy," Angel explained.

No one took what Angel said very seriously, especially the part about the fruit-colored lipstick. Penguin said only monsters used lipsticks like that.

Mo couldn't stand it any longer. He smacked Penguin in the stomach! How dare he call his mother a monster? Mo had to protect his mother's name.

Penguin rubbed his stomach and moaned loudly. Seeing this, Monkey and Hippo went over to sympathize with Penguin. Mo was a bit shocked to see how much he seemed to have hurt Penguin. His stomach must have been full of air!

But Penguin was just pretending to be hurt while waiting for a chance to get back at Mo. He threw himself at Mo and headbutted him in the stomach.

Now it was Mo's turn to moan. Angel quickly

checked to see if Mo was all right.

Mo had fought with lots of boys in class, including Hippo and Monkey, but he had never fought with Penguin before.

Monkey began to play referee. He held up Penguin's hand and Mo's and said, "Would the two contestants like to continue the fight?"

Monkey and Hippo both hoped that Penguin and Mo would carry on so they could enjoy the spectacle.

But neither Penguin nor Mo wanted to fight. They only wanted to prove whose mom was the prettiest mom in the whole wide world.

"That's easy." Monkey could always be relied on to come up with ideas. "Let's set up a time for Penguin's mom and Mo's mom to get together. Then we can ask several people to be judges, so that they can judge the two moms side by side."

"Who will be the judges?"

Monkey pointed at himself with his thumb. "Of course, me, and Hippo . . ."

Those two wanted to be judges? Both Penguin and Mo thought they weren't good enough to judge their moms.

"Not just the two of us, of course," Monkey said. "We can ask Man Man and Lily to be judges too. Two guys and two girls, perfect!"

"I don't want Man Man to be a judge," Mo objected. Man Man was Mo's desk-mate and she always voted against him on everything. Mo was sure Man Man would vote in favor of Penguin's mom.

"Okay, we'll ask Lily and Angel to be judges," Monkey said.

"I don't want Angel to be a judge," Penguin immediately objected.

Everyone knew that Angel was Mo's neighbor and that she adored Mo. She would definitely vote in favor of Mo's mom.

Mo knew that Angel would vote in favor of his mom too. But Mo was also confident that his mom would win, so he wanted a fair competition.

"All right, we'll ask Lily and Man Man to be judges," Mo said.

Now that everyone had agreed to the judges, they had to think of a way to get Penguin's mom and Mo's mom to meet up.

Again, it was Monkey who came up with an idea. "You two were fighting earlier. What do you think will happen if we tell Ms. Qin?"

"She'll ask our parents to come to school!" both Mo and Penguin shouted together.

MONKEY'S WISE IDEA

Monkey asked Angel to tell Mo's desk-mate, Man Man, that Mo and Penguin had been fighting.

As soon as Man Man learned of the fight, she immediately told Ms. Qin. So Ms. Qin asked both Mo and Penguin to go and see her in her office.

Seeing Mo in trouble again, Ms. Qin sighed. "Mo, if I could have one day where I don't see you in my office, it would be worth a big celebration with fireworks."

"Ms. Qin, fireworks are no longer allowed in the city," Mo said very seriously.

"I know, and don't you lecture me, young man."

Ms. Qin knew that there was no point in getting angry with Mo. He was a troublemaker, but he had a good heart.

Ms. Qin turned her attention to Penguin. Unlike Mo, who had to report to her office almost every day, Penguin only reported to her office every two or three days.

"Penguin, why were you fighting with Mo?"

"Because Mo smacked my stomach."

"Penguin poked my stomach too," said Mo.

As Mo said this, he took off his belt and was going to take off his pants too. He wanted Ms. Qin to see the red marks on his stomach.

"All right! All right! I believe you, Mo. Now put your belt back on at once." Ms. Qin really didn't feel like seeing Mo's stomach.

"So, what should I do with you two?" she asked.

"Ask our mothers to come to school," Mo and Penguin said at the same time. Now, Ms. Qin did not expect that answer. She was going to ask the two of them to write one hundred lines: "I must not fight with other boys."

"Fine, if you insist!" Ms. Qin thought it was indeed

time to see their parents to discuss how the boys had been behaving lately.

"When will you ask them to come?" Mo and Penguin said simultaneously again, sounding anxious.

Ms. Qin thought this rather strange. "When do *you* want me to ask them to come?"

"As soon as possible!" replied both boys.

Ms. Qin had penetrating eyes that could see through everything. She stared at Penguin and then at Mo until both of them turned red.

"Fine, I will ask them to come tomorrow afternoon!"

"All right!"

As soon as Mo and Penguin left Ms. Qin's office, they gave each other a high five, which *of course* did not escape Ms. Qin's eyes.

What are those two up to? she wondered.

The two boys were so happy that they forgot they hadn't yet asked Man Man to be one of the judges.

"Man Man, we'd like to invite you to be our judge," Penguin said very nicely.

"To judge what?" replied Man Man cautiously.

"To judge which of our moms is the prettiest mom in the whole world."

"Don't you two have better things to do with your time? How about studying, for example?"

"It's okay if you *don't* want to be our judge," Mo said. He knew how to hit Man Man right on her weak spot. "As long as we have Lily as our judge, it will be fine."

When Man Man heard that Lily had agreed to be their judge, Man Man insisted on becoming their judge too. She couldn't lose to Lily. Besides, Man Man didn't believe that Mo's mom was prettier than

Penguin's mom, because Penguin's mom was very pretty. If Mo's mom was so pretty, how could she have given birth to someone as ugly as Mo?

As soon as Mo got home that day, he told Honeybunch that Ms. Qin wanted her to go to the school tomorrow.

"Mo, have you gotten into trouble again?"

"I had a fight with Penguin."

"Well, I don't want to go to your school. I have work to do," said Honeybunch. "Your father will have to go."

Honeybunch really didn't want to go and see Ms. Qin. She remembered how Ms. Qin lectured Mo's dad every time he went to Mo's school. Honeybunch couldn't bear the thought of Ms. Qin lecturing her like a little kid if she went to see her.

"But you must go. Dad is away!"

Mo was right. Mr. Ma was on a business trip away from home.

Honeybunch was annoyed. "Mo, give me a break. Okay, if I must go in and see Ms. Qin, I will."

"Mom, one other thing. You must look really pretty tomorrow when you come to my school."

Honeybunch laughed. "Mo, I'm going to school to be scolded by your teacher. I'm not entering a beauty contest."

"But Mom, if you look really pretty tomorrow, Ms. Qin won't scold you."

Honeybunch wasn't in the mood to listen to Mo's nonsense, but Mo was being very insistent. He carried on with his pleading.

"When you go to school tomorrow, will you wear the hair comb I bought for you on Mother's Day? And will you wear your beautiful dress with the phoenix pattern on it, please?"

"Mo, what is going on here . . . ?"

"Mom, let me tell you a secret. When our teacher Ms. Qin sees very pretty people, she becomes speechless. And if she's speechless, she won't be able to say anything bad about me!"

The following day, Honeybunch wore what Mo had asked her to. She looked really pretty when she went to see Ms. Qin in the afternoon. Ms. Qin was so surprised when she saw how pretty Mo's mom was. She could not believe Mo had a mother as beautiful as a princess.

Honeybunch not only surprised Ms. Qin, she surprised Penguin's mother as well. Penguin's mother thought she was like a beauty queen, but when she saw Honeybunch with her pink lip gloss, her Pisces hair comb, her phoenix-patterned dress, and her calf-leather boots, she was amazed.

Penguin's mother asked Mo's mother what her job was. She thought perhaps she was a model.

"I am a showcase designer. I design store windows."

"Oh, how fantastic. I was looking for a store window designer." Penguin's mother immediately grabbed Honeybunch by the arm and said, "I am about to open a store and I am looking for someone to design its windows."

Penguin's mother and Mo's mother were talking so much and so quickly that Ms. Qin could not get a word in. Finally, Ms. Qin had to ask the two mothers to discuss their business opportunity somewhere else, because they were disturbing the other teachers in the office.

Honeybunch went off with Penguin's mother in her red Porsche. When Mo, Penguin, and the four judges—two boys and two girls—ran out of the classroom to look for them, all they could see was a red Porsche speeding out of sight. So no one won the prettiest mom contest, but Mo's mother was happy that she'd been to his school after all.

MAN OF THE HOUSE

Before he went away on his next business trip, Mo's father wanted to talk to Mo about something important.

"Mo, come here and take a seat. There's something I need to talk to you about."

"It's okay, Dad, I can listen to what you have to say standing up." Mo was playing darts. He was aiming for the bull's-eye with one eye closed.

Mo's father raised his voice. "Mo, this is serious."

"If Mo doesn't want to hear it, I will," said Honeybunch as she walked into the room and sat on the sofa across from her husband.

"Honeybunch, this is a man-to-man talk. Could you give us a minute?"

Mo was still mumbling with one eye closed, "Why does a man-to-man talk have anything to do with me?"

"Man-to-man means you and me." Mo's father thought this was getting funnier by the minute. "Mo, are you a man or not?"

Mo walked over like a man and sat down with an air of confidence like a man.

Mo glanced at his father and couldn't help but giggle. Mo was very used to his dad's teasing. Now that Mr. Ma had put on a very serious look, Mo just couldn't take him seriously.

"Mo, I'm going on a business trip to Europe. I will be visiting seven countries—"

"Countries in Europe are small. Visiting seven countries is like visiting seven cities here," Mo interrupted rudely.

Mo had heard this from Penguin. Last summer, Penguin had gone on a tour of Europe with his parents. In seven or eight days, he visited eight countries. Each country took him just one day to visit.

"Let me finish," said Mo's father quickly. "I will be gone for quite a while this time—about a month. If I'm not here, there is only one man left in the house."

Mo looked around for this man his dad was talking about.

"I mean YOU." Mr. Ma patted his son's head. "Do you know what *responsibilities* the man of the house has?"

The man of the house obviously had lots of responsibilities, but Mo didn't know where to start.

"Let's only talk about a man's responsibilities at home: to protect his wife and children and give them a sense of security."

"But I don't have a wife and I don't have children—" Mo said.

Mo's father knew where Mo was headed, so he quickly cut him off. "That's right. You don't have a wife and children now, but you will someday. Right now, you have Honeybunch. Honeybunch is a woman and all women need protection."

Mo patted his father on the head. "Don't worry, Dad, as long as I'm here, Honeybunch won't be scared."

Mr. Ma asked Mo, "Do you know what Honeybunch is scared of?"

"Mice."

"What else?"

Mo didn't know.

"Storms," said his father.

"Really? I didn't know she was afraid of thunder."

"Not thunder, lightning. I've just looked up the weather forecast on the internet, and it looks like there will be thunderstorms while I'm away."

Mr. Ma looked very worried. Whenever he looked worried, his eyebrows drooped. Mo knew he was really serious.

★

The following day, Mr. Ma had to catch a very early flight. Before he left, he dragged Mo out of bed. "Mo, I am leaving now. You're in charge of this family while I'm away."

Mo was still half asleep and couldn't even open his eyes properly. Mr. Ma held Mo's hands and looked very serious. "Mo, I am leaving Honeybunch for you to take care of."

Mo couldn't really see or hear anything. As soon as his dad let go of his hands, he fell right back into bed.

There was a thunderstorm that very same night. The

sky went pitch-black, occasionally lit up by flashes of blinding lightning.

"Open up all the curtains, Mo!" Honeybunch said happily. "Now that your dad is not home, I can finally enjoy watching the lightning."

"But I thought you were afraid of lightning," Mo said.

"Your dad told you that, didn't he?" Honeybunch laughed. "The truth is, it's your dad who's afraid of lightning. I have to pretend to be even more afraid of it to make him feel better. Men forget their own fears when they are protecting their loved ones."

Honeybunch walked to the window and looked at the lightning in the sky. "Look, it's just like fireworks. I love it when there's lightning in the sky."

Mo stared at the lightning for a long time and could see how dramatic it was. But he was a bit disappointed. He thought he could protect his mom when lightning came, but it turned out that she wasn't afraid of lightning at all!

Suddenly, there was a particularly bright fork of lightning in the sky—it lit up Honeybunch's face, making her look like a ghost.

Eek! Mo gave a scream and almost fainted.

So now Honeybunch had to protect Mo from the lightning!

NOISES IN THE NIGHT

Honeybunch pretended that she was afraid of lightning so her husband could feel strong and protective. But when it came to mice, Honeybunch was *not* pretending. She really was terrified of mice. Her hands and feet turned icy cold and her hair stood up on end if ever she saw a mouse.

Mo rubbed his hands excitedly. Now he would be able to protect Honeybunch.

"Honeybunch, I promise that while Dad is away, you will not see a single mouse."

Honeybunch was amused to see Mo acting like

the man of the house.

"Mo, you're my child, not my husband. You don't have to protect me or make promises like that."

Mo spoke even more seriously. "It's a promise from a man to a woman."

Honeybunch laughed so hard that her stomach hurt. Mo didn't think it was funny at all. After all, he *was* the man of the house now.

There were mice in the apartment complex, that was a fact. Mo sometimes heard Honeybunch's screams in the kitchen when she discovered mouse droppings.

But though there were mouse droppings, they had never found any mice. Those loathsome mice—where could they be hiding?

Mo decided to investigate. He would do a complete search of the apartment. He would scare the mice by making a very loud noise with his soccer noisemaker!

Taa taa taa! Taa taa taa!

Mo spun the noisemaker all around Honeybunch's bed!

Taa taa taa! Taa taa taa!

Taa taa taa! Taa taa taa!

Mo spun the noisemaker around every corner of the apartment, especially the kitchen.

But the mice didn't seem to be scared of the noisemaker. They still left droppings in the kitchen. Mo had an idea.

"If I can't take care of those mice, I'll find someone who can."

The "someone" Mo was thinking about wasn't a person, but a dog called Hotdog. Hotdog was a very old dog with lots of creases, so he looked like a very old man. The dog rarely looked happy and he was always sniffing around the apartment complex. But when he saw a mouse, Hotdog always looked really happy. No mouse had ever escaped from his paws. Although Hotdog didn't eat mice, he did give them a really hard time. Once a mouse got into his hands (or rather, paws), it would beg to be eaten instead of played with. . . .

Hotdog's owner always called him "Good Boy," but Mo always called him "Old Boy" because he wasn't particularly good at all. At first, Hotdog never used to answer Mo's call, but after a while, when Mo called out "Old Boy," the dog sometimes came to him.

"Old Boy! Old Boy! Come here, Old Boy."

Old Boy frowned and gave Mo an uninterested glance.

Mo threw a crumpled piece of paper at Old Boy.

Old Boy sniffed at the paper. There were mouse droppings inside.

Old Boy sniffed the mouse droppings and dashed toward Mo like greased lightning, wagging his tail furiously. Mo took Old Boy back to his apartment. Old Boy checked each room, sniffing the entire time. When he got to the kitchen, Old Boy went berserk.

Grrrrr! Grrrr!

Woof! Woof!

Old Boy barked really loudly at the kitchen ceiling. In a few moments, the sound of scuttling could be heard.

"Go get them!" Mo shouted at Old Boy.

But Old Boy was only a dog, and there was no way he could get up to the ceiling.

The louder Old Boy barked, the faster the mice ran around above them. Now that even Old Boy was out of ideas, Mo had no choice but to shut the kitchen door tight so that the mice couldn't get into the other rooms.

In the middle of that night, Mo suddenly

woke up. He got out of bed and went to the kitchen to make sure the door was safely closed.

His parents' bedroom was on the way to the kitchen. Mo could hear a funny grinding sound. He thought it must be the noise lots of mice make when they're chewing something.

"Oh no. Those mice are inside the bedroom!"

Mo grabbed his noisemaker in one hand and a flashlight in the other and sneaked into Honeybunch's bedroom.

The sound of mice was getting louder.

"How dare those mice! Wait till I get them!"

Mo crawled on the floor and checked underneath the wardrobe and the bed, but there was nothing. But Mo could still hear the grinding sound of mice.

Mo could see that the curtains were moving. He crawled over and checked the curtains and then every corner of the room. But there were no mice.

Grind . . . Grind!

Grind . . . Grind!

Mo listened closely and realized the sound was coming from the bed.

Did this mean the mice were on Honeybunch's bed?! How horrible! If Honeybunch knew there were

mice on her bed, she'd have a heart attack!

The grinding sound continued. Mo checked the bed everywhere with his flashlight, but he didn't see any mice.

Did this mean the mice were underneath the blanket? The thought of it gave Mo goose bumps.

Mo pulled Honeybunch's blanket away.

"Ahhhhhh!"

A loud scream scared Mo half to death. He fell onto the floor, dropping his noisemaker and his flashlight.

Honeybunch sat up looking horrified. She turned on the light and saw Mo on the floor. "What on earth are you doing, Mo?!"

"I thought I heard mice in here."

"Mice?" Honeybunch cowered under the blanket as soon as she heard the word. "Get rid of them, Mo, hurry up!"

"I can't find them, but I heard the sound of mice grinding things in their mouths."

Mo imitated the sound he had heard. Honeybunch laughed and laughed and then said, "That was me making that noise. I was grinding my teeth."

"Grinding your teeth? Why would you do that?"

"Some people grind their teeth in their sleep. But Mo, there's no need for you to tell anyone." Honeybunch made Mo promise he wouldn't go telling any of his friends that his mother ground her teeth at night. They might think she was some kind of monster!

There was no way Mo was going to tell anyone. After all, his mother was the prettiest mom in the whole world. He wasn't going to let anyone know what noises she made in her sleep.

Mo may have been mischievous, but he certainly wasn't stupid!

SiLVER, HiGH-HEELED SANDALS

Mo and Honeybunch went shopping together most weekends.

Honeybunch loved shopping, especially at the Shopping Center because she loved looking in all the store windows, some designed by her.

Suddenly Mo started laughing. He saw a whole store window full of fake legs.

The store was supposed to be displaying women's shoes, not fake legs. But Mo didn't see it like that, of course! All the fake legs in the window wore beautiful leather shoes: high-heeled shoes, medium-heeled shoes, low-heeled shoes, and platform shoes. But it was a pair of silver high-heeled sandals that caught Mo's attention. They reminded him of the crystal slippers from *Cinderella*, the crystal slippers he'd said he wanted to buy for his mother when he was older.

"Look, Mom, you should buy those!" said Mo to Honeybunch.

"But I don't like wearing high heels," Honeybunch said.

Honeybunch liked to wear shoes with no heels because they were the most comfortable for walking.

Mo said, "But Dad says women should wear high heels. Just look at all the models you see in magazines, they all wear high heels. Ms. Lin wears high-heeled shoes too."

Ms. Lin was Mo's art teacher. Mo thought she was the prettiest teacher in the whole world.

Mo dragged Honeybunch into the shoe store and tried to make her buy the pair of silver high-heeled sandals.

 105

But Honeybunch said she was just not comfortable wearing high heels, and she hadn't even worn high heels for her wedding to Mo's father.

"Please, please wear high heels just this once, for me!" Mo pleaded.

Honeybunch knew that when Mo insisted on something, he wouldn't stop unless she agreed. So she went into the store and bought the pair of silver high-heeled sandals.

The heels on the shoes were very high and Honeybunch felt as if she were walking on stilts. She didn't dare take many steps. She made Mo hold her hand so she could keep her balance.

"Mo, I don't think I can walk in these sandals. I'd better just take them off!"

But Mo didn't want Honeybunch to take the sandals off. "Honeybunch, you look even prettier in those shoes. You are the prettiest mom in the whole wide world."

Honeybunch didn't want to let Mo down. She held on to Mo and stumbled along the pavement looking in more store windows.

Honeybunch walked half a block with great difficulty. But she gradually got used to the shoes and when she could walk by herself, Mo let go and went to see things that were more interesting to him.

Suddenly he heard Honeybunch cry out:

"Mo!"

Mo turned around and saw Honeybunch sprawled on the pavement.

"It's my ankle. *Ouch!* I think it might be broken." Honeybunch's ankle hurt so much she wanted to cry.

Mo had to get his mom to the hospital. But they were on a pedestrian-only shopping street, so there weren't any taxis. Mo thought about giving Honeybunch a piggyback ride, but luckily realized that was out of the question. Then Mo had an idea. He remembered when he'd sprained his ankle once, he managed to hop to school on his good foot. Mo was always very good at hopping. So Mo told Honeybunch that she would have to hop to the hospital. (Mo nearly said *hopital*, but he didn't think Honeybunch would find it funny at that particular moment!)

Mo and Honeybunch hopped together. They hopped out of the pedestrian-only shopping street, they hopped to the taxi stand, got into a taxi, and went to the hospital. The doctor said that Honeybunch had a soft-tissue injury to her ankle. It wasn't very serious, but it was very painful. The doctor said that they could treat her ankle with a special ointment that should help it to heal. Unfortunately, injuries to the ankle usually took at least three months to heal completely, which meant for the next three months, Honeybunch had to return to the hospital several times for treatment.

Honeybunch knew that Mo felt sorry about the whole thing even though he didn't say anything. If Mo hadn't insisted that Honeybunch buy the pair of silver high-heeled sandals, and hadn't insisted that she wear them while shopping, Honeybunch wouldn't have had the accident.

★

When they got home, Mo told Honeybunch she should put her feet up and rest. Then he went out to the supermarket to buy her some pork shanks. The doctor had told him that pork-shank soup was good for healing soft-tissue injuries.

At the supermarket, fresh pork and beef were all in packets and placed neatly on the meat shelf.

Mo didn't know what pork shank was and he was

also very worried about leaving Honeybunch on her own for too long. He said to some of the other shoppers, "My mom has an ankle injury, and I need to buy pork shanks for her."

An old lady picked a packet of pork shanks for him and asked whether he knew how to make pork-shank soup.

Mo said he didn't know how to cook anything except instant pot noodles.

So the old lady told Mo her secret recipe for pork-shank soup.

On his way back home, Mo kept reciting what the old lady had told him again and again. He didn't dare think about anything else because he was afraid he would forget the recipe for pork-shank soup.

It was actually quite simple: After the pork-shank bones have been washed clean, put them in a big pot and add water. Bring the water to a boil and then throw it away. Then wash the pork-shank bones again, add water, and boil it up again. When the soup boils this time, turn the heat to low and let the soup simmer till it turns white. When the soup is as white and creamy as milk, it's ready.

Mo kept so busy in the kitchen that his face turned red and his forehead was all sweaty. All the time, Honeybunch kept calling Mo to do little errands for her.

"Mo, I need to go to the bathroom."

"Mo, I need to take my medicine."

"Mo, could you get me get those magazines from the table?"

Mo was overwhelmed, but he was beginning to feel like the man of the house because Honeybunch needed him to take care of her; Honeybunch couldn't live without his help.

It took three hours for the pork-shank soup to turn as white and creamy as milk.

Honeybunch only had one sip and already she could tell the soup was very special. "Mo, did *you* make this soup?" she asked.

"You thought I could only make pot noodles, I know," Mo said.

Honeybunch put down her soup bowl and said, "Somehow I feel that you're not like the Mo I used to know."

"Who else could I be?" said Mo with an innocent look on his face.

The phone rang. It was an international call from Austria from Mo's father.

"Hello, son, is everything okay with Honeybunch?"

The first thing Mr. Ma asked about was Honeybunch. To him, Honeybunch always came before Mo.

"She's doing fine," replied Mo.

Mo didn't dare tell him that Honeybunch had hurt her ankle. Otherwise his dad would fly back from Austria immediately.

Mo was confident that he could take care of Honeybunch. In fact, it felt great to be needed by someone. For the first time ever, Mo felt that he could really be the man of the house.

MO GETS JEALOUS

On Monday morning, Mo wanted to call school to take a day off. He wanted to look after Honeybunch. He also wanted to go to the hospital with her for her next treatment. But Honeybunch refused to let Mo take a day off from school. She said she could go to the hospital by herself.

"But you can't even walk. How are you going to get there?" Mo asked.

"I have my crutch!" Honeybunch said. "I can walk there with the help of the crutch."

But Mo didn't think this was good enough. He said

to Honeybunch, "Do you prefer the crutch to your son?"

"The crutch is the crutch, and my son is my son. You cannot compare the two. If you insist on taking a day off from school, then I will refuse to go to the hospital."

Honeybunch's threat worked like magic. Mo agreed to go to school, but he still wasn't sure about letting Honeybunch go to the hospital with just a crutch for support. Mo found a piece of paper and a felt-tip pen and wrote the following:

PLEASE HELP MY MOM. THANK YOU!

When Mo helped Honeybunch put on her coat, he secretly taped the piece of paper to the back of it.

Mo and Honeybunch went out the door together. Mo headed toward school and Honeybunch headed toward the hospital with the help of the crutch. Mo turned back and took one more look at the piece of paper taped on Honeybunch's back. He felt relieved.

On her way to the hospital, lots of people asked Honeybunch whether she needed help.

Honeybunch was so touched. People were so nice these days!

A few people actually volunteered to escort Honeybunch to the hospital. Seeing that these nice people all had jobs to go to, Honeybunch told them she would be fine by herself.

Finally, an old man riding a bicycle insisted on giving Honeybunch a ride to the hospital.

"Go ahead and get your injury treated. I'll wait for you right here," the old man said.

Before Honeybunch had the chance to thank the old man, other people offered to help her walk into the hospital. The old man kept his word and waited outside for Honeybunch to return.

"Let me give you a ride home!" the old man said.

Honeybunch couldn't remember how many times she said "thank you" that day. When the old man took Honeybunch home, he finally said, "Don't thank me, thank your child!"

"My child?"

Honeybunch had no idea what the old man meant.

"Is your child a boy or a girl?"

"Boy."

"How wonderful to have a son like that!" The old man pulled off the piece of paper from the back of Honeybunch's coat. "He must be such a good boy!"

Honeybunch recognized Mo's handwriting right away.

★

Meanwhile, at school, Mo found it was impossible to focus on his work. What if Honeybunch needed to go to the bathroom? What if she needed to get a drink of water?

He couldn't wait for the end-of-school bell to ring so that he could go home and take care of his mother.

As soon as the bell rang, Mo raced out like a hurricane. He ran as fast as he could. He had to rush home to take care of Honeybunch and to make her pork-shank soup. As his father wasn't at home, he was the man of the house. It was his job to look after his mother.

"Honeybunch, I'm home!" he yelled from the front door.

But when he went into the apartment he saw a large bouquet of lilies in the crystal vase on the living room table. Lilies were Honeybunch's favorite flowers.

Only Mo's father gave lilies to Honeybunch. Did that mean his father was home? Mo wondered.

"Dad! Dad!"

"Your dad hasn't returned yet," said Honeybunch, who was resting on her bed.

"But the lilies . . ."

"Ah, those—my boss asked someone to send those to me."

"Your boss with the big beer belly?"

Mo had seen Honeybunch's boss once at a Christmas party. He dressed himself up as Santa Claus and carried a huge sack of presents on his back. He gave the presents away to anyone he ran into. The boss looked really silly, like a bear dressed in a Santa Claus costume.

"How does that silly bear know you like lilies?" Mo couldn't get over the fact that Honeybunch's boss had sent her lilies. He thought only he and his dad knew about Honeybunch's favorite flowers.

"Mo, that wasn't very nice. You mustn't call him a silly bear. Anyway, he's coming to the apartment later. Make sure you greet him properly."

"Why does he need to come here? He's already sent you flowers."

 117

"He bought some pork shank, so he said he will bring it over after work."

What? Flowers and *pork shank?*

Mo thought it was his job to take care of Honeybunch and make pork-shank soup for her. Why should someone else get in on his act? It wasn't fair!

The doorbell rang. Mo knew it must be the beer-belly boss.

Mo went to the door. Before he opened it, he squeezed a soccer ball behind the door so that the door would only open halfway.

"You must be Mo!" Beer-Belly Boss tried squeezing inside the door as hard as he could. "Sorry to keep you waiting!" he puffed.

Yeah, right! Who did he think was *waiting* for him?

Beer-Belly Boss tried very hard, but he still couldn't squeeze through the door. Mo was trying hard not to laugh, but he managed to look cool and told the boss to take a deep breath!

The door was stuck on the boss's big beer belly. Beer-Belly Boss sucked his breath in so hard that his eyes were almost bulging out of their sockets, but he still could not get through the door.

"Just a little more! You're almost there!" encouraged Mo, stifling a giggle.

Seeing that Beer-Belly Boss was trying his hardest, Mo had another idea. He took out the soccer ball wedged behind the door. The door suddenly flung wide open, and with a loud crash, Beer-Belly Boss fell forward and crashed into the display case where Mo's mom had put the twelve-layer sandwich for everyone to admire. His head hit the case and smashed the glass. Bits of sandwich went all over his face, and Beer-Belly Boss soon had a big lump on his head too.

"Mo! How could you! You must apologize AT ONCE." Honeybunch had seen everything while she was trying to walk over to the front door with her crūtch. She was furious with Mo.

When Beer-Belly Boss finally left, Honeybunch was still very upset. She was also still mad at Mo.

"Mo, why did you do such a thing? Your father asked you to look after me, not make my life a misery."

★

Mo couldn't even explain himself. He had tried so hard to be the man of the house, but sometimes things just didn't quite work out the way he wanted them to. Perhaps he still had a lot to learn. It was tough being a boy, especially a boy as mischievous as Mo, a boy with so many ideas! But one day, he knew, just like his father, he would get everything right!

READERS' NOTE

MO'S WORLD

Mo Shen Ma lives in a big city in China. Modern Chinese cities are very much like ours, so his life is not so different from your own: he goes to school, watches television, and gets into mischief—just like kids all over the world!

There are *some* differences, though. Chinese writing is completely unlike our own. There is no alphabet, and words are not made up of letters—instead, each word is represented by a little drawing called a *character*. For us, learning to read is easy. There are only twenty-six letters that make up all our words! But in Chinese, every word has its own character. Even Simplified Chinese writing uses a core of 6,800 different characters. Each character has to be learned by heart, which means that it takes many years for a Chinese student to learn to read fluently.

NAMES

Chinese personal names carry various meanings, and the names in this book have definitely been chosen for a reason! Take Mo Shen, the hero of our tale. His name is made up of the words *Mo*, which means "good ideas" and *Shen*, which means "deep" or "profound." So you can see how much his name suits him, because Mo Shen is always coming up with great ideas!

STORY BACKGROUND

You might have noticed that neither Mo nor any of his classmates have any siblings—and as a result, they all have to plan Mother's Day on their own! In fact, being an only child is the norm in China. This is due to a government-led initiative called the Planned Birth policy (usually referred to outside of China as the "one-child policy"). Since the 1970s, all parents in China have been encouraged to have only one child, in an effort to restrict overpopulation and foster a healthy economy.

A lot of people have criticized the one-child policy. Some people think the one-child policy has created a generation of "little emperors" because so much attention and care are lavished on one child by two parents and four grandparents! What do you think? Is Mo a little emperor? Or does he have a heart of gold underneath his mischief-making?

Enjoy more of Mo's Mischief
with this sneak peek at

PESKY MONKEYS

THE BIG BLACK CAT
AND
THE BIG WHITE CAT

Mo Shen Ma was on his way to Grandma and
Grandpa's house for summer vacation. Mo's grandparents lived at the foot of a big mountain in the
countryside that was also a nature reserve. Lots of rare
and protected species lived on the mountain.
Grandma always shut the garden gate as soon as it got
dark. She said there were wild tigers on the mountain

that liked to carry away small children in their mouths and eat them in their mountain dens.

Mo thought Grandma was only trying to frighten him, because he'd never seen a wild tiger, and he explored all around Grandma and Grandpa's house whenever he went there to visit.

As soon as Mo's dad's car stopped, an old white goose came over, swaying from side to side and honking as if to greet them.

When Mo and his dad got out of the car, they heard someone shouting, "We have guests!" But Mo didn't recognize the voice. Who was it?

Grandpa and Grandma hurried out to greet them.

"Guests?!" Grandma said, looking up. "This is my son and my grandson. They're not guests! They're family!"

Mo looked up too, wondering who his grandma was talking to. A birdcage hung in the porch of the house, and in it was a brown, yellow-beaked bird.

"That's Grackle," said Grandma. "He always speaks when he sees people. Don't you, Grackle? He's *much* better than a parrot."

"Thank you! Thank you!" said Grackle, nodding vigorously.